Dònal Ò

the Cocky kooster

BOOK FIVE OF THE DÒNAL ÒG SERIES

by

Donal McCarthy

Illustrations by Emily Fuhrer

Website: **DonalOgSeries.com**

Joshua Tree
Publishing

• Chicago •

Dònal Òg and the Cocky Rooster

Book Five of the Dònal Òg Series

by Donal McCarthy

Published by
Joshua Tree Publishing
• Chicago •
JoshuaTreePublishing.com

13-Digit ISBN: 978-1-956823-07-3

Credits: All Illustrations by Emily Fuhrer
Website: **DonalOgSeries.com**

Disclaimer:

Printed in the United States of America

Dedication

To my daughters
Cara, Ashling, and Níamh
and my grandaughters
Eden and Aria

Thank You
Emily Fuhrer
Ami on Vancouver Island
John Paul Owles

Dònal Òg and the Cocky Rooster

Dònal Òg stood backed up against the trunk of the tree with his heart pounding so hard that he thought Ma could hear it all the way inside the cottage. In his hand, he held a long branch of a blackthorn tree that he was using to fight off a very angry, determined rooster. In all his seven years, he had never hated or feared anything as much as this demonic bird.

As it charged at him again with an outstretched head and gaping beak, he thought it couldn't be much smaller than an ostrich, a bird he had just read about in a storybook. It stood almost as high as his knees, had a deep-red comb on its head that got darker and taller when it was angry.

Right now, it seemed to be nearly taller than Dònal Òg himself. Its red eyes seemed to be on fire as it flew into the air and tried to get to him.

That's enough, thought Dònal Òg. *I have had enough. I am going to teach this devil a lesson.*

With that, he started flailing at it with his blackthorn branch, hitting it again and again until it backed off.

Then he chased it down the yard, still hitting it as hard as he could. No longer as confident as it was a moment ago, the rooster fled in panic as blows rained down across its back and head. All the fear and anger that Dònal Òg had been feeling was being directed into each blow.

It was unfortunate that it was at that moment that Ma should walk around the corner of the cottage. The first thing she saw was an out-of-control Dònal Òg seemingly attacking an innocent fowl.

"Leave my poor cock alone!" she cried. "You will be the death of him. What's wrong with you? I ask you to bring in a few fresh eggs for breakfast, and all you do is attack the chickens."

No amount of explaining helped. Ma had seen what she had seen, and she wasn't happy.

"Really, Dònal Òg," she said. "You better start being more responsible, or I will have to have a chat with the fairies." This was the most serious threat that Ma could make. Everyone knew that you didn't want the fairies paying attention to you.

It's just not fair, thought Dònal Òg to himself. *Next time, I will let it kill me, then she will be sorry.*

Gathering up the eggs from under the clucking hens, he was feeling quite sorry for himself. Then his dog Rover bounded up to him and rubbed itself on his legs. This lifted his spirits immediately but set off an uproar among the hens. They both escaped out of there and left the hens in a foul mood.

When he got to the kitchen, his cousins Aria and Eden were already at the breakfast table, chattering away happily. They were telling Ma all about their adventure in the enchanted woods. She was listening with half an ear while she pondered on why Dònal Òg would want to injure or kill her favorite rooster—it was so out of character for him.

Just then, Eden said, "Ma, did you see how the rooster was attacking Dònal Òg just now? We thought it was going to peck him until he was full of holes. He was very brave to chase it away."

Ma felt very guilty. He had tried to explain, but she hadn't listened. She gave Dònal Òg a big hug and said sorry. If the rooster ever chased him again, they would have it for Sunday lunch. Dònal Òg felt very happy. The threat of the fairies had been lifted.

Standing outside in the sunshine, Dònal Òg, Eden, and Aria wondered what to do with the rest of the day. "I know," said Eden. "Let's try to catch some baby rabbits. We can also see if we can find baby pheasants. We can put them in with the hens, and next year, we will have our own big pheasants."

Crossing the yard was tricky these days. They now had three angry creatures that they had to avoid. The first and most dangerous was the nanny goat. It had become angrier the older it became. It charged without any warning every chance it got. Dònal Òg thought he would ask Ma if they could have the goat for Sunday lunch as well. Remembering that Da said that the nanny goat was Ma's mother that had been changed into a goat by the fairies, Dònal Òg thought that maybe that would make her sad, so he wouldn't do that. Then there was the half-naked turkey that he had tried to catapult over the shaking bog from the top of a tree. It hadn't worked out so well. Now, the turkey chased him every time it saw him. Added to that list was the angry rooster.

He thought to himself, *I hope Da won't buy a big bull.*

Dònal Òg had his catapult in his hand as he and his cousins ran across the yard. If anything chased them, they were going to regret it, he thought. They made it into the green field safely. Nothing was interested in them, it seemed.

As they walked along the riverbank, they saw a herd of cows grazing quietly in the field. They were small black cattle. Dònal Òg knew that they were a breed called Kerry cattle, a rare breed first brought to Ireland in ancient times. Da said that they were brought here by wandering Celts about 2,000 years before the birth of Jesus. Da said that they gave the best amount of milk of any of the cattle breeds.

Dònal Òg was happy that Da was happy, but he secretly wished that he didn't have to fetch their cow from the field in the morning. Even on summer mornings, the grass was damp and cold, and as he had no shoes, his feet were always really cold when it was his turn to fetch the cow.

A deep bellow, followed quickly by another deeper one, alerted Dònal Òg, Eden, and Aria to the fact that the bull was loose in the next-door field. They peered through the hedge and saw to their horror that the bull was coming toward them at full speed, all the time bellowing furiously. With no time to lose, they turned and ran back toward the cottage, reaching the gate in record time. Climbing over it and standing behind it, they heaved a sigh of relief.

"What a lucky escape!" said Aria. "That bull was really cross."

"Did you see the big ring in its nose?" said Eden. "That means it's a really bad bull. Let's not say anything to Ma, or she will stop us from having adventures."

They all agreed.

Suddenly hearing thudding hooves behind them, they turned around to see the nanny goat charging toward them with its head down and the largest set of horns that Aria had ever seen (she really hadn't seen many goats or horns).

"Quick!" shouted Dònal Òg. "Climb back over the gate!"

They did in quick time. As they stood there, shaking in their shoes between a large angry bull and a smaller angrier goat, Eden had a great idea. "We should open the gate a little and let the goat chase the bull, and as soon as the goat comes through the gate, we can close the gate while jumping back over it."

They all thought it was a great idea, especially as the bull, having found a hole in the hedge, was now in the same field as they were. They opened the gate just a little and allowed the goat to charge through. Quick as a flash, they were up and over the gate and pulling it closed behind them. They now were safe at last. Dònal Òg didn't say anything, but he was now worried about the nanny goat. If the bull killed the goat, they would be in big trouble for letting it into the field with a dangerous bull. He also thought that if it was Ma's mom, she would be very sad. Then the strangest thing happened: the nanny goat charged straight up to the bull and stopped right in front of it.

"That's the end of it," all three of them said to each other, referring to the goat.

"That huge bull is going to toss it straight up in the air with its long, pointed horns," said Eden.

They closed their eyes and waited for the cries from the goat. They never came. Opening their eyes again, they saw the bull and the goat rubbing noses.

Soon they were the best of friends and grazing in the field together. Seeing them standing and looking over the gate, Ma joined them and got the shock of her life.

"Well, I never!" she exclaimed. "I have heard it said that the lion will lie down with the lamb, but this beats it all."

Dònal Òg, Eden, and Aria had no idea what she was talking about, so they ran away to play again. Now that the back of the cottage was closed off to them by both the bull and the goat, they had to find a new route to the riverbank.

"Let's go down to the bridge," said Eden. "We can climb down from there."

As they walked along, they peered into the furze bushes and the hedges, looking for bird nests. Eden found one in a hole where a branch had broken off an alder tree. It was made from grass, moss, and dead leaves. The bowl was lined with wool and soft feather down.

"That's a robin's nest," said Dònal Òg. "I found eggs in one last year, and they were pale blue with brown spots."

Both girls hoped that they could also find one. Then they found a thrush's nest low down on a shrub, made of twigs, grass, and moss. It was held together by mud. Also, the inside was lined thickly with the same mud. Aria wondered how a bird was able to make the inside so perfectly smooth without hands.

"The fairies help them," said Dònal Òg. The explanation was accepted by the girls as the only one possible.

Down in a boggy patch near the riverbank, the yellow flag iris was in full bloom. Its long sword-like leaves made perfect boats for their boat races on the river. The masses of yellow flowers stood out among all the greenery. Eden wondered why so many plants were yellow in Ireland. Dònal Òg didn't think there were that many.

"Well," said Eden. "Let's count all the ones we can think of."

Aria said, "Me first!" so they had to agree. "I saw furze bushes," she said, "then buttercups."

"Dandelions and cowslip," said Eden. "Also, daffodils and primroses."

Dònal Òg found this very boring. Flowers were just flowers to him. It seemed silly to call them all different names, just more stuff to learn and difficult to spell. *Why not just call them all flowers?* he thought. *It's difficult enough to remember them in English, but I will have to learn them in Irish as well. Then I will also have to learn to spell them in two languages.* It was enough to take the joy out of his day for a moment.

A loud splash took his mind off the problem. A pair of wild ducks had landed in the river. From their colors, he knew that they were mallards. The male had a blue-green head, brownish body, and an upturned tail. The mottled brown one, he knew, was the female.

Da had explained to him that the females had to be a drab color, as they had to blend into the nest when they were hatching their eggs. Soon they both had their tails in the air as they searched for food underwater. Dònal Òg thought that all the small fish would have darted away as soon as the two monster heads appeared underwater. He thought it must be like a giant sticking its head in through his bedroom window.

A squeal from Aria brought him back to the banks of the river. She had seen the white bobbing tail of a rabbit in the field. They got down on all fours and crept stealthily in the direction where she had seen it.

Suddenly there in front of them were many rabbits, lots of babies and quite a few adults. They lay quietly in the grass and watched the little ones at play.

The adults continued eating, every now and again looking around and sniffing the air to make sure there was no danger. Hawks and foxes were their biggest enemy, swooping in and carrying off a baby or even an adult in the blink of an eye.

Dònal Òg felt a sneeze coming on. Before he could help it, the silence was shattered by the explosive sound. "ATCHOO!" Faster than you could say the word, the meadow was empty, not a rabbit to be seen anywhere. Just like that! The ducks blasted off the water and, in a twisting low flight, soon disappeared. They had the river and the field to themselves once again. They lay there in the grass a little longer, listening to birds singing and bees droning.

A few fields away, he could hear the farmer speaking to his horse as he guided him around the field, pulling a hay rake. The sun had been shining for weeks now. The first long grass had been cut and was now turning into hay.

All three drifted off to sleep and woke up to find a herd of curious cows staring down at them.

A mother cow seemed to be telling her calf to look and see what happened when you wandered away from your mother.

Dònal Òg wondered if the fairies and the cows communicated with each other. Every time he fell asleep in a field, he seemed to wake up with cows staring at him.

"Don't be silly," said Aria. "It's because cows live in fields, and we don't. If you found a cow asleep in your bed, you would also stare."

He thought she had a point, but a cow would never fit into his bed.

At the top of the hill, the enchanted woods seemed to be calling them. Eden and Aria wanted to go there and talk to the little trees. They had a lot of fun with them when they last visited. Dònal Òg thought it might make the fairies cross if they kept bothering them. He had only been in the enchanted woods twice in his life before he took the girls there.

The first time, he had wanted to take some of the beautiful small red apples to eat. This was before he knew that only fairies were allowed to pick and eat them. As he had reached up to pick the reddest juiciest one, a big black crow had dive-bombed him and chased him away. Then a flock of starlings had flown over, and one had pooped on his head.

The second time, he had tried to rob the eggs from a bird's nest. A big owl had flown straight at his face. He felt that it was only because he was faster than the light from his torch that it hadn't bitten off his nose. So no, he was in no hurry to return there.

Yes, the last time, everything had gone well. Eden and Aria said it was because he behaved himself and didn't try to do anything to upset the fairies or anything else that lived there. *Boring!* he thought to himself.

Up the hill, they climbed and soon stood at the hole in the hedge leading into the enchanted woods. They peered inside without making any noise. They didn't want to disturb any sleeping fairies. They saw a beautiful butterfly with red wings that had large bright-blue eyes on each one. When it sat on a flower, you thought that it was looking at you. Ma had told him that it was called a peacock butterfly and that the false eyes were to scare anything away that was trying to eat it. Then on a nettle bed, they spotted a dark-brown one with red stripes and white patches. It was a red admiral, he knew.

He told the girls what Ma had told him. If he had said what it was without mentioning Ma, they wouldn't believe him.

So busy were they watching the butterflies dancing back and forth from plant to plant that they didn't see or hear anything else. Then suddenly they heard a shy hello. Looking around, they couldn't see anyone else. Then Eden spotted a leaf moving on a fairy finger or foxglove plant. Then a tiny, winged fairy that looked just like a damselfly popped out of one of the purple tubes that were the flowers.

"Hello and welcome!" she said. "Would you like me to show you around?"

"That would be every kind of you," said Eden. "We would be happy if you would."

"You are so pretty," said Aria. "I wish I could look like you!"

Dònal Òg nearly swallowed his tongue. Everyone knew that you should never make a wish to a fairy. They always feel obliged to grant you your wish. He didn't know how he would explain to Ma when he brought Aria home the size of a damselfly, especially as she had warned them again and again not to trouble the fairies.

Quick as a flash, he spoke loudly and said to the fairy, "I wish I was as clever as you." He knew that a second wish, if spoken immediately, would cancel out the first one.

He was very relieved to see that Aria stayed her normal size. He waited a little while to see if he felt any cleverer. No, nothing was happening.

Maybe I got one that isn't more clever than I am, he thought. Then a terrible thought entered his mind. What if she is less clever than I am? he thought. I asked her to make me as clever as she is! Hopefully, she is not the dummy of the fairy fort. Cold sweat broke out on his forehead.

That's what comes of troubling the fairies, he could already hear Ma saying as she had to teach him to read and count all over again. He would have to learn how to tie his shoelaces, spell, and do his seven times tables. He was overcome with fright and had to sit down. He closed his eyes and recited his seven times tables, counted from one to forty-two, and undid and retied his laces. He felt very happy when he discovered that he could still do it all. He thought it would be a good idea to get out of the enchanted woods before anything else could go wrong. After all, his cousins just weren't used to dealing with fairies. He wasn't either and would like to keep it that way for as long as possible. Da always said that you should never shout at the devil; that way, he wouldn't take any notice of you.

As he mused on all of this, the girls were chattering away with the fluttering fairies. As they zoomed and zipped around just like a butterfly, they pointed out all the different flowers and berries to the girls.

The fairies explained what they were used for, which ones were good for them, and which ones they shouldn't touch.

Just then, a big fat frog sitting on a lily pad saw it fluttering about. Thinking it would make a delicious meal, it shot its tongue out and nearly caught the fairy. Quick as a bolt of lightning, the fairy aimed its magic wand at the frog and turned it into a slimy slug. A crow darted down and swallowed it in one gulp.

It's really time to get out of here, thought Dònal Òg again. *This could get nasty.*

Luckily just then, they heard Ma calling that it was time to come home. He thought he saw a frown appear on the fairy's face and realized that it had been leading them deeper and deeper into the enchanted woods. Any later, and they wouldn't have been able to find their way out before sunset. He knew that they would then have been put under a spell by the fairies and forced to stay there until the sun came up again. As the fairies would have taken them underground, that could be forever and ever. Hearing Ma's voice, the fairy knew that it had to lead them back to the edge of the enchanted woods.

This shouldn't happen, thought Dònal Òg. We have an agreement with Queen Niàmh. I will tell Aunt Tess. She will know what needs to be done.

Waving goodbye to the fairy, they headed off homeward. The sun was beginning to drop toward the mountains in the west, painting the sky orange. Soon it would disappear behind them before sinking into the sea and sending a blaze of pink shooting skyward. All of this was going around in his mind. He should have been paying more attention to more worldly things.

Hearing a shriek from Eden brought him back to reality. The rooster was racing straight toward them, neck outstretched, and wings held wide. Its intent was clear—revenge on the dreadful creature that had caused him to sit and stew all day after the humiliation visited on him in the morning.

In less time than it took to write this sentence, Dònal Òg whipped his catapult out of his back pocket, took aim, and sent a small round stone hurtling in the rooster's direction.

Then a miracle happened. For the first and—I can tell you here and now—the last time, his aim was true.

The rooster stopped dead in its tracks and dropped like a rock. *Thud!* So loud did it sound in Dònal Òg's ears that he thought Ma had heard it for sure.

In the blink of an eye, he raced up to the now-dead rooster, grabbed its legs, and heaved it over the hedge into the wildly flowing Doughlasha. Watching it being swept along on the flow, he said, "Good riddance." They thought it best not to mention anything to Ma. Da always said that in most situations, the lesser said, the better. He felt that Da was the wisest person he knew, so he would take that advice.

Soon Uncle Danny was playing a cheerful jig on his accordion. The children danced around the floor while the adults looked on, smiling. Out of the twilight came the most unearthly sound. Ma made the sign of the cross and grabbed her rosary beads. She was convinced that someone was returning from the dead. When Da went outside to check, she turned out to be right, even if she didn't know it. There stood a wet, bedraggled, sorrowful-looking rooster. Dònal Òg's stone hadn't killed it, just stunned it.

When it landed in the cold water, it was washed up on a mudbank and soon recovered. Ma just stood there, looking at it and saying, "Whatever is the matter with that bird, it's time it went in the oven for Sunday lunch." Dònal Òg couldn't agree more.

So ended the day for Dònal Òg. Soon he was sleeping soundly and dreaming of the forests lying buried deep in the bogs. He was helping Da pull some of them out of the deep mud when one started talking to him.

But that's a story for another day.

The End

READ THE DÒNAL ÒG SERIES

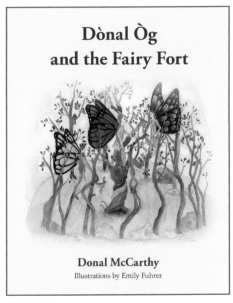

BOOK ONE

BOOK TWO

Dònal Òg is a young boy growing up in the rural Irish countryside in the 1950s. These are the tales that were told in front of a glowing peat fire that the family would gather around on the dark winter nights. It was before the invention of television, so people made their own entertainment. Belief in the fairy folk was strong amongst the people, especially the children. The tales carried many suggestions on how to behave and included many warnings on the consequences of breaking those rules. As a boy with a very active imagination, **Dònal Òg** took it all to heart.

These are his stories.

Website: DonalOgSeries.com

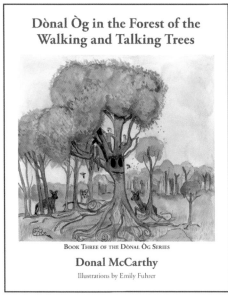

Book Three

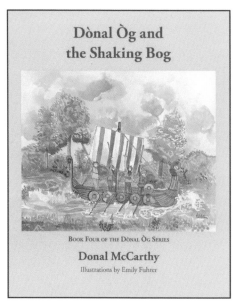

Book Four

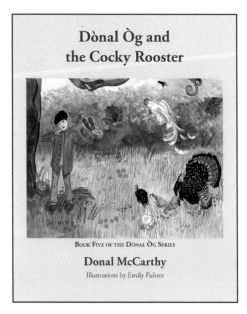

Book Five

Printed in Great Britain
by Amazon

81791269R00022